MAY 2018

min**edition**

English edition published 2018 by Michael Neugebauer Publishing Ltd., Hong Kong

© Utopique 2014 - Hameau de Teillol - 19380 ALBUSSAC - FRANCE

Text Copyright © 2017 Emmanuel Bourdier

Illustration Copyright © 2018 ZAÜ

English translation rights © 2018 Michael Neugebauer

The original French edition "Les Jours Noisette" was published 2014 by Éditions Utopique - http://utopique.fr/

Rights with UTOPIQUE éditions, Didier JEAN & ZAD, Albussac, France

Unit 28, 5/F, Metro Centre, Phase 2, No.21 Lam Hing Street, Kowloon Bay, Kowloon, Hong Kong.

Phone +852 2807 1711, e-mail: info@minedition.com

This edition was printed in July 2017 at L.Rex Printing Co Ltd.

3/F., Blue Box Factory Bldg, 25 Hing Wo Street, Tin Wan,

Aberdeen, Hong Kong, China

Typesetting in Avenir Next Condensed

Library of Congress Cataloging-in-Publication Data available upon request.

ISBN 978-988-8341-54-2

10 9 8 7 6 5 4 3 2 1

First Impression

For more information please visit our website: www.minedition.com

HAZELNUT DAYS

Emmanuel Bourdier

Illustrated by ZAÜ

minedition

It's two o'clock.

Today Dad smells like peppermint. I prefer it when he smells like hazelnut.

Grandma gave Dad two bottles of cologne. One has a hazelnut fragrance, which smells like a nice, breezy forest. The other is peppermint–which smells like my school's bathroom.

I tell him that if he keeps using that fragrance, someone will flush the toilet and he'll disappear down the drain.

He tells me that if he uses the hazelnut he runs the risk that a mob of squirrels will leap all over him. He chuckles at that, his one gold tooth flashing. Hearing him laugh like that makes me feel warm inside.

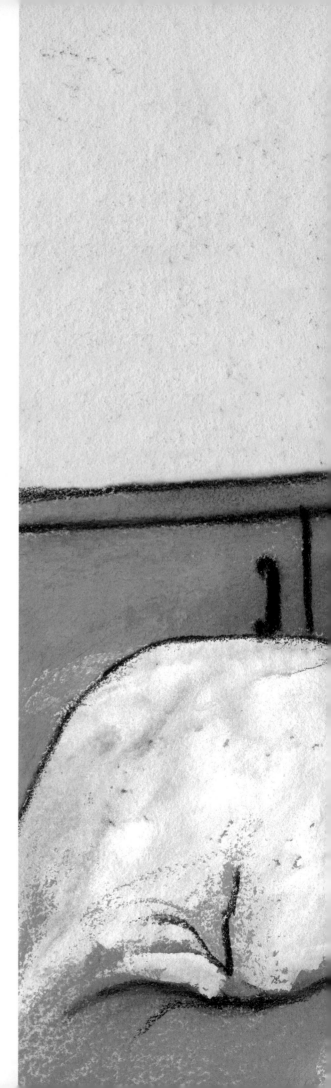

Aside from the peppermint I can also smell cigarettes. Dad has started smoking again—already the third time this month.

Last time I warned him he could get cancer, and I crushed his pack of cigarettes. He got really mad—a deep, quiet anger without any yelling. But his eyes turned red, and his hands squeezed into white fists.

This time I don't crush anything. But I still disapprove.

At the beginning when my school friends asked me,
"What job does your Dad have?" I wasn't quite sure what
to say. So I said nothing and found myself alone under
the big lime tree in the schoolyard, just staring at the sand.

Now I tell them: He's a cloud sculptor, a mole tamer, an
inventor of dirty words.

They laugh at that, and the sound of their laughter rises
through the tall branches.

But at the same time he's also:
a void maker,
a ghost king,
a fog machine.

I know my Dad and I belong together when I look at his ears.

We're the only ones in the world who can wiggle our ears up and down and wag them from side to side.

And we can both touch our tips of our noses with our tongues. Well, a lot of people can do that. But the ear trick is something only we can do.

One day we'll race each other to see who's the fastest, and I'll win.

By then he'll be too old to catch me.

When I'm with Mom I never use the word "Dad." When-ever we start talking about him, we call him "Cave Bear." That suits him well because of the hair on his back. On the way here I asked her how she first met Cave Bear.

She said that one summer day he crashed into her car in a parking lot. The rest is history.

I told her it would have been wonderful if she'd had another child with him. She said she'd rather have just one child like me with him than eight other kids with some stranger.

The lady sitting next to us had a sour look on her face. She didn't like our conversation.

I try not to show him my report cards. I've warned him that he won't like them, but he's as stubborn as a donkey and demands to see them.

My grades in math are bad enough, but when he sees my marks in language, he hits the roof. He grabs my arm so tightly it hurts. He tells me I have no right to do so poorly in school—it's my only chance to avoid becoming like him.

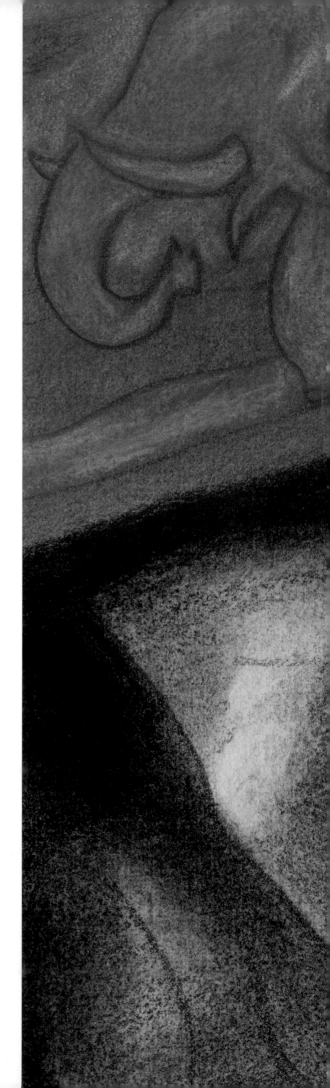

Sometimes I hate Dad when I see Mom's sad eyes.

But I don't mind her scared eyes when there's a thunder-storm outside. When she crawls into bed to calm me down, she hugs me, our feet peeking out from under the blanket. She sings me lullabies, though her voice trembles.

It makes me feel warm inside, and then I love thunder-storms. This is what I call happiness.

If I hate Dad, it's because of the fog in Mom's eyes.

A kind of fog that arises when she looks through his
small, square window. It's as if her eyes are clouded by
dull weather. There's nothing to see in them—just a blank
white sky.

Dad pretends not to notice it, but everyone knows he's
the cause of it.

Fog machine.
Yes, in such moments I hate him.

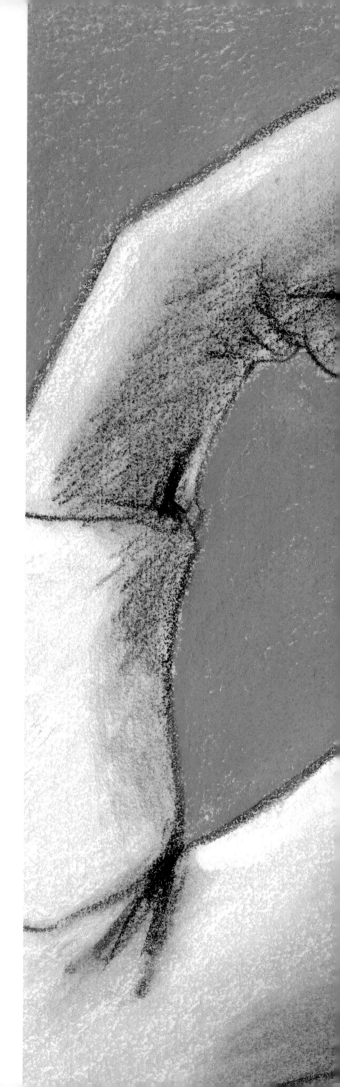

Dad is strong–very strong. When he flexes his muscles a big round lump appears on his arm. I think it's great. I think Mom likes it, too.

And he can be so funny. He can imitate all kinds of people–especially my Aunt Kiki.

And he was on a TV show once. Say what you will, but one day I want to be like him.

Except for the peppermint–that goes too far.

Today Dad imitates a sparrow. He squeezes his nose, closes his eyes,
and lets out a series of high-pitched chirps.

When he finishes he looks really proud of himself. He tells me how
you can find sparrows all over the world, even in the smallest parks.
You just need to know how to use your eyes and ears.

The guard with the whistle around his neck cackles. He says Dad's
bird imitation sounds like a sick, old crow.

Dad pretends not to hear him. I don't like this guard.
He's mean, and he certainly doesn't know
how to use his ears properly.

Dad begins to cry.
Once again.
I wonder if he cries less when he smells like hazelnut.
I think so.

I don't cry with him—not this time.

It's three o'clock now.

Visiting hours are over.

The guard gets out his giant, jangling key ring.
That's how I know our time is over.

Before we leave the visitor's room I kiss Dad on the
cheek. Deep beneath the peppermint he smells just
like him. Not like prison, not like the stale walls, not
like cigarettes.

I'll try to keep that smell in my nose the whole week.

And next week I'll bring him hazelnuts.
An extra-large bag.

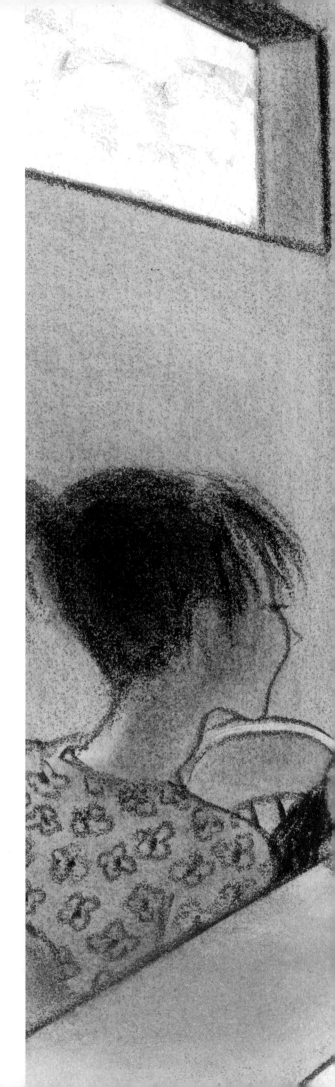